This book belongs to

_____

_____

This edition published by Parragon Books Ltd in 2014

Parragon Books Ltd
Chartist House
15–17 Trim Street
Bath BA1 1HA, UK
www.parragon.com

ISBN 978-1-4723-8311-2

Printed in China

DISNEP MOVIE COLLECTION
A SPECIAL DISNEY STORYBOOK SERIES

From the movie
DISNEP
FROZEN

PaRragon

Bath · New York · Cologne · Melbourne · Delhi
Hong Kong · Shenzhen · Singapore · Amsterdam

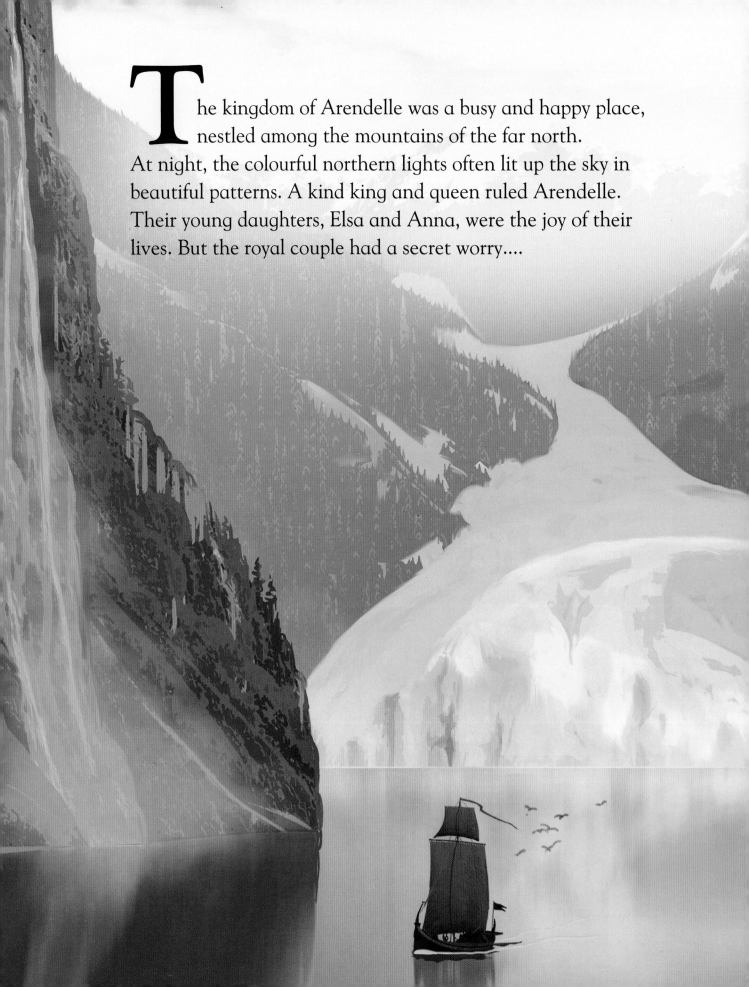

The kingdom of Arendelle was a busy and happy place, nestled among the mountains of the far north. At night, the colourful northern lights often lit up the sky in beautiful patterns. A kind king and queen ruled Arendelle. Their young daughters, Elsa and Anna, were the joy of their lives. But the royal couple had a secret worry....

Their eldest daughter, Elsa, had a magical power.
She could create snow and freeze things with her hands!

Anna, the younger daughter, adored her big sister. The two were inseparable. One night, Anna convinced Elsa to sneak into the Great Hall in the castle and create a winter wonderland!

But while the girls were playing, Elsa accidentally hit Anna with a blast of icy magic. Little Anna fell to the ground, shivering. A streak of white appeared in her hair. Frightened for her sister, Elsa called out for help.

The worried king and queen rushed their daughters to the realm of trolls. The trolls were mysterious healers who knew about magic.

A wise old troll spoke to them. "You are lucky it wasn't her heart that was struck," he said. "The heart is not so easily changed, but the head can be persuaded. We should remove all magic, even memories of magic, to be safe."

The old troll was able to cure Anna by changing her memories and removing all magic from her mind. This meant she wouldn't remember Elsa's magical power.

The troll warned the king and queen: "Fear will be your enemy."

Back in Arendelle, the king and queen felt more worried than ever. They locked the castle gates and taught Elsa to control her powers so that no one would find out about them. But whenever she had strong feelings, the magic spilled out.

So the king gave her a pair of
gloves to help hold it back.
  Elsa decided that to keep
Anna safe, it would be best to stay
away from her.

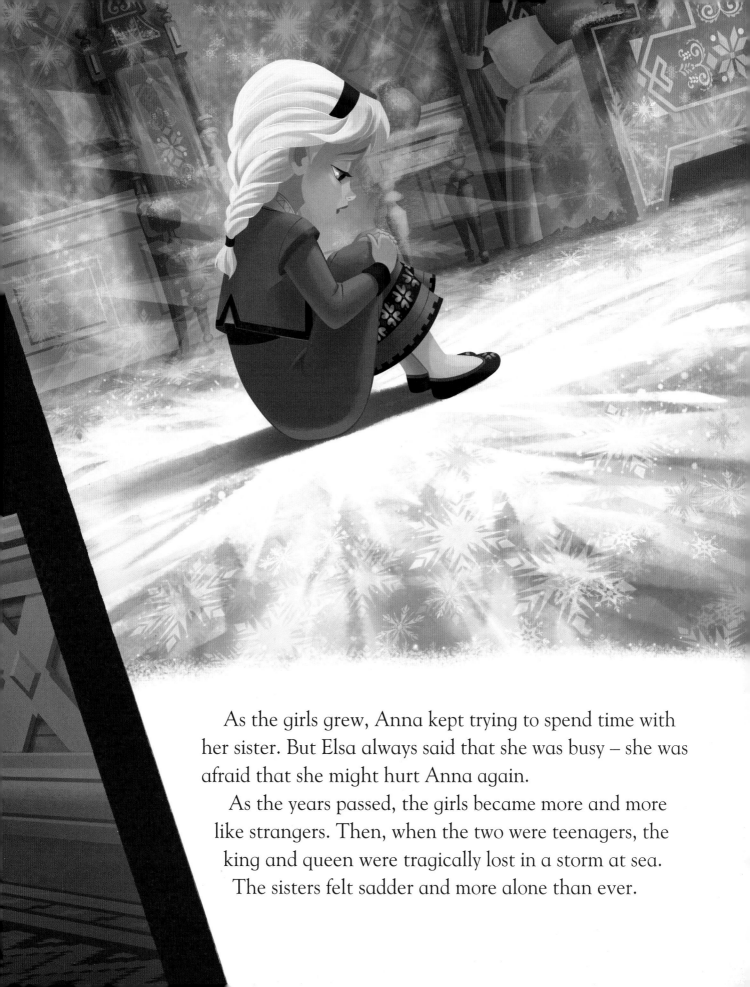

As the girls grew, Anna kept trying to spend time with her sister. But Elsa always said that she was busy – she was afraid that she might hurt Anna again.

As the years passed, the girls became more and more like strangers. Then, when the two were teenagers, the king and queen were tragically lost in a storm at sea. The sisters felt sadder and more alone than ever.

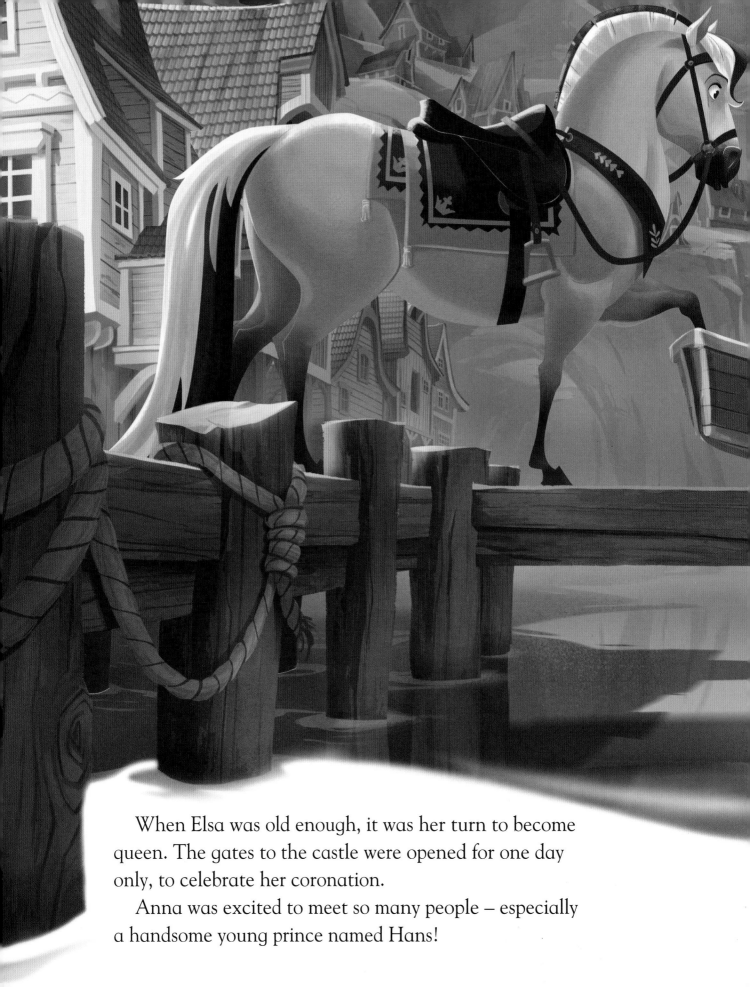

When Elsa was old enough, it was her turn to become queen. The gates to the castle were opened for one day only, to celebrate her coronation.

Anna was excited to meet so many people – especially a handsome young prince named Hans!

But Elsa was still struggling to hide her powers.
She just hoped that she could make it through the
day without anybody finding out about them.

To Elsa's relief, the celebration went
exactly as planned. Everybody cheered for
their beautiful new queen.

Afterwards, a party was held in the
Great Hall. Anna and Prince Hans spent
the evening laughing, dancing and talking.
They had so much in common! Everything
seemed perfect, so they made a big decision....

Anna introduced Hans to Elsa – and announced that they were going to be married.

Elsa was shocked. "You can't marry a man you just met," she told Anna.

"You can if it's true love," Anna insisted.

But Elsa would not listen to Anna's arguments. "My answer is no," she said firmly. "The party is over!"

Elsa started to leave the room, but Anna grabbed her hand – she was trying to make Elsa stay and talk. But Anna accidentally pulled off her sister's glove!

Anna kept arguing. She was confused and angry.
"Why do you shut me out?" she asked Elsa. "I can't live
like this anymore!"

"Enough!" Elsa cried. An icy blast shot from her uncovered hand, sending a sheet of ice across the ballroom! Everyone stared in disbelief.

Elsa fled the castle, devastated that her secret had finally been revealed and terrified that she might hurt someone. "Stay away from me!" she warned the townspeople.

Everything around Elsa turned to ice as she ran.
She stepped onto the fjord and the water froze solid!
She raced towards the mountains on the other side.

Elsa climbed into the mountains, and with nobody around to
worry about, she let all of her power loose for the first time.
As she neared the top of the mountain Elsa created a
magnificent, shining ice palace. She felt free!

A blizzard flew around her. She even transformed
her own dress into a beautiful icy gown.
At last, she felt like the person she was always
meant to be!

Elsa's blizzard had covered Arendelle with snow and everyone was panicking because it was the middle of summer. Anna knew that she had to find Elsa to thaw out the land – plus, she wanted her big sister back. Now that Elsa's secret was out, they could finally be close again!

Leaving Hans in charge of the kingdom, Anna rode into the mountains. The storm made the journey difficult, though, especially when Anna's horse threw her into the snow. Luckily, she spotted a small building up ahead.

The building was Wandering Oaken's Trading Post
and Sauna. Anna rushed in and immediately gathered
up some supplies.

A young man named Kristoff was also collecting
winter supplies. He mentioned that the storm was coming
from the North Mountain.

Anna began asking questions. If the storm was on the North Mountain, Elsa would be there, too!

But Kristoff was busy bargaining for supplies. Feeling crowded, he finally blurted out, "Now back up, while I deal with this crook!" The insulted shopkeeper threw him out empty-handed into the snow.

This gave Anna an idea. She found Kristoff in the stable with his reindeer, Sven, and offered to give him the supplies he needed. In return, she asked that he take her up the North Mountain.

Finally, Kristoff agreed. "We leave at dawn."

"No," said Anna. "We leave right now."

Anna and Kristoff climbed onto a sledge and Sven began pulling them up the mountain.

At first the journey was quite pleasant. Anna told Kristoff all about Elsa and what had happened in Arendelle.

But suddenly, a pack of wolves began to chase them! Anna helped Kristoff to fight off the wolves. Eventually Sven was forced to leap across a deep gorge to escape the fierce creatures.

The sledge crashed onto the rocks below, but Anna, Kristoff and Sven were safe.

The trio continued into the forest on foot. They soon came across a beautiful winter scene. Anna was more eager than ever to find Elsa – she had to know more about her sister's amazing power!

"I never knew winter could be so ... beautiful," Anna said.

"But it's so white," added a voice. "How about some colour?" It was a living snowman!

"I'm Olaf," he said, explaining that Elsa had made him.

Anna gave Olaf a carrot nose, then asked him to lead them to her sister. "We need Elsa to bring back summer."

Olaf grinned. "I've always loved the idea of summer,"
he said. "The warm sun on my face, getting a gorgeous tan.
Just doing whatever snow does in summer."

But Anna and Kristoff were both thinking the same thing:
summer would not be a good thing for a snowman.

The path up the mountain grew more and more difficult. Luckily, Olaf soon found a stairway made of ice leading straight to Elsa's palace.

"Whoa," exclaimed Anna in awe as they reached the top. The palace was amazing!

They approached the front door and Anna knocked. After a moment, the door swung open.

Elsa was worried to see Anna. She wanted to return home with her sister, but she knew that everything would be different now that her secret was out. She also remembered how dangerous her powers could be.

"I think you should go, Anna," Elsa said. "I'm sorry. It has to be this way."

But Anna explained that Arendelle was still frozen. If Elsa stayed away, everyone in the kingdom would freeze to death!

Now Elsa was scared. She admitted to Anna that she didn't know how to undo her magic.

Anna was sure that they could work it out together, but Elsa thought that was impossible. It crushed her to know she was still a danger to others.

Elsa's feelings overwhelmed her until her powers burst out of her – and struck her sister in the heart!

Anna still refused to leave, feeling certain that she could still help her sister. But Elsa insisted – and conjured up a giant snowman to escort Anna outside, along with Kristoff and Olaf.

"Hey, you made me a little brother," Olaf said to Elsa happily. He turned to the huge snowman. "I'm going to name you Marshmallow!"

Elsa ordered Marshmallow to escort Anna and her companions off the mountain. But after Anna hit him with a snowball, he decided to chase them, instead!

The friends ran until they reached a cliff and then lowered themselves down the side. But Marshmallow grabbed the rope and pulled them back up. Anna did the only thing she could think of – she cut the rope!

Luckily, Anna, Kristoff and Olaf landed safely in a soft
snowdrift down below. But something was wrong with Anna –
her hair was turning white!

"What happened back there? What did she do to you?"
Kristoff asked.

Anna explained that Elsa had struck her with her powers.
Kristoff knew just what to do. He had some friends who were
experts at just about everything. They could help Anna!

Night fell as Kristoff led Anna and Olaf to the realm of trolls. Seeing Kristoff, the trolls came out of hiding. Kristoff had spent a lot of time with them as he grew up, so he was practically family!

When an old troll touched Anna's hair, he understood immediately that she had been hurt. "There is ice in your heart, put there by your sister," the old troll said. He explained that Anna would freeze to solid ice forever in one day's time unless the magic was reversed. "Only an act of true love can thaw a frozen heart."

Thinking quickly, Olaf and Kristoff decided to take Anna back home. Surely, Prince Hans could break the spell with a true love's kiss.

Back in Arendelle, Hans had become worried when Anna's horse had returned without her. So he had gathered volunteers to help him find Anna.

When Hans's group arrived at the ice palace, Elsa tried to protect herself. But in the struggle, she was hit by falling ice and knocked out. She ended up being taken back to Arendelle as a prisoner.

Kristoff and Anna were unaware of what had happened at Elsa's ice palace. Kristoff took Anna to the castle gates at Arendelle and sadly passed her over to the servants. He was starting to realize that he cared deeply about Anna. But he knew she was in grave danger ... and that her true love, Hans, would be able to make her well again.

The servants built a fire in the library to warm Anna, but still she was getting colder by the minute.

Anna was so glad
when Hans arrived.
She explained what
Elsa's icy blast had
done and how a true
love's kiss could cure
her. "Only an act of
true love can save me,"
she said.

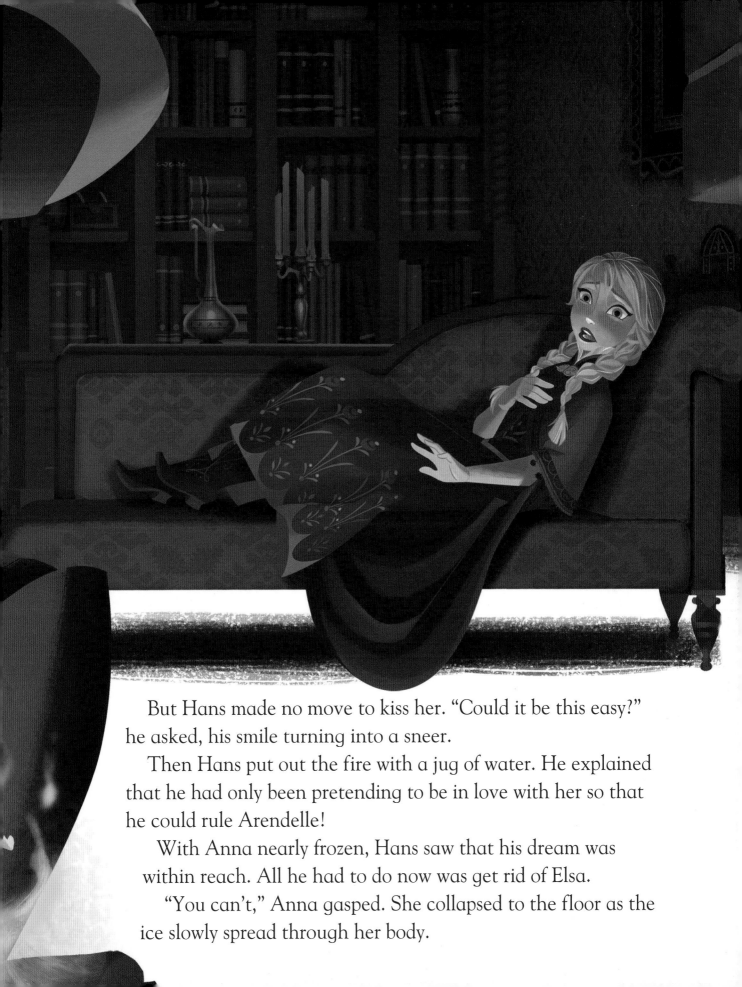

But Hans made no move to kiss her. "Could it be this easy?" he asked, his smile turning into a sneer.

Then Hans put out the fire with a jug of water. He explained that he had only been pretending to be in love with her so that he could rule Arendelle!

With Anna nearly frozen, Hans saw that his dream was within reach. All he had to do now was get rid of Elsa.

"You can't," Anna gasped. She collapsed to the floor as the ice slowly spread through her body.

Meanwhile, imprisoned in the castle dungeon, all Elsa could think about was getting away from the kingdom, to protect everyone from her powers. She was also worried about Anna – she didn't know that Anna was back in Arendelle, too.

Elsa became so upset that she lost control of her magic and froze the dungeon. The ice broke her chains and she escaped!

At that same moment, Olaf helped Anna to get to her feet and come outside. The little snowman had realized that Kristoff loved Anna – and that his kiss could save her!

Anna spotted Kristoff running over to her and she began to move slowly towards him, almost completely frozen. But then, she saw something else – Hans was about to strike Elsa with his sword!

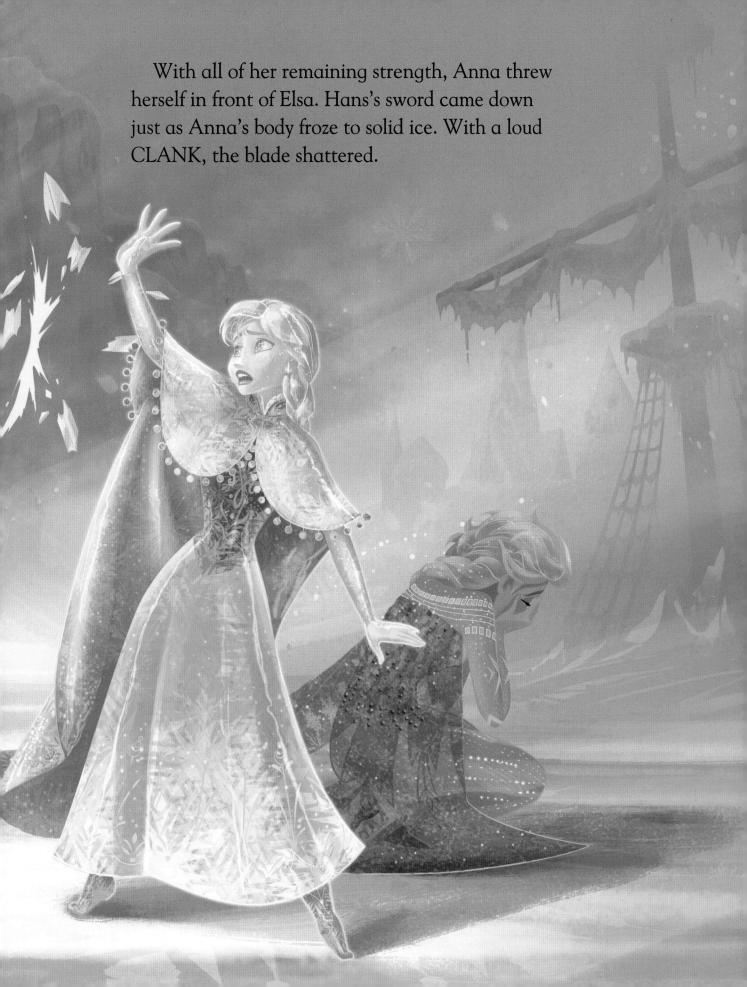

With all of her remaining strength, Anna threw herself in front of Elsa. Hans's sword came down just as Anna's body froze to solid ice. With a loud CLANK, the blade shattered.

Elsa wept as she wrapped her arms round her sister. "Oh, Anna," she sobbed.

A moment passed. Then something amazing happened. Anna began to thaw!

"Elsa?" Anna whispered.

"You sacrificed yourself for me?" Elsa asked. Anna nodded weakly.

"An act of true love will thaw a frozen heart," Olaf said.

With her sacrifice, Anna had helped Elsa to see that love was more powerful than fear.

Suddenly, Elsa realized that love was the force that could control her powers. She raised her arms and the ice and snow that covered Arendelle melted away.

But Olaf was melting, too! Elsa quickly made a little snow cloud just for him.

"This is the best day of my life!" he said.

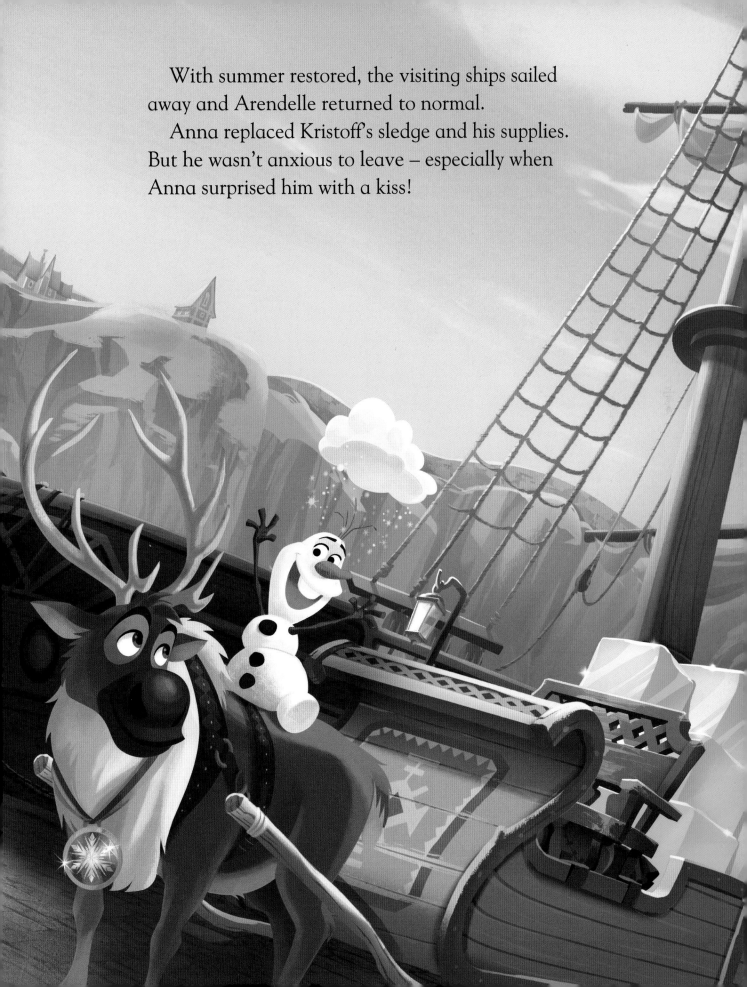

With summer restored, the visiting ships sailed
away and Arendelle returned to normal.

Anna replaced Kristoff's sledge and his supplies.
But he wasn't anxious to leave – especially when
Anna surprised him with a kiss!

Elsa created an ice-skating
rink in the castle and threw open
the gates of the kingdom – she never
planned to close them again.

Everyone had a wonderful time skating with
Queen Elsa and Princess Anna. The kingdom of Arendelle
was a happy place once more!

Anna and Elsa
knew that they would never
let anything come between them again.

From the movie

Disney

FROZEN

An Amazing Snowman

Written by Barbara Jean Hicks

illustrated by Olga T. Mosqueda

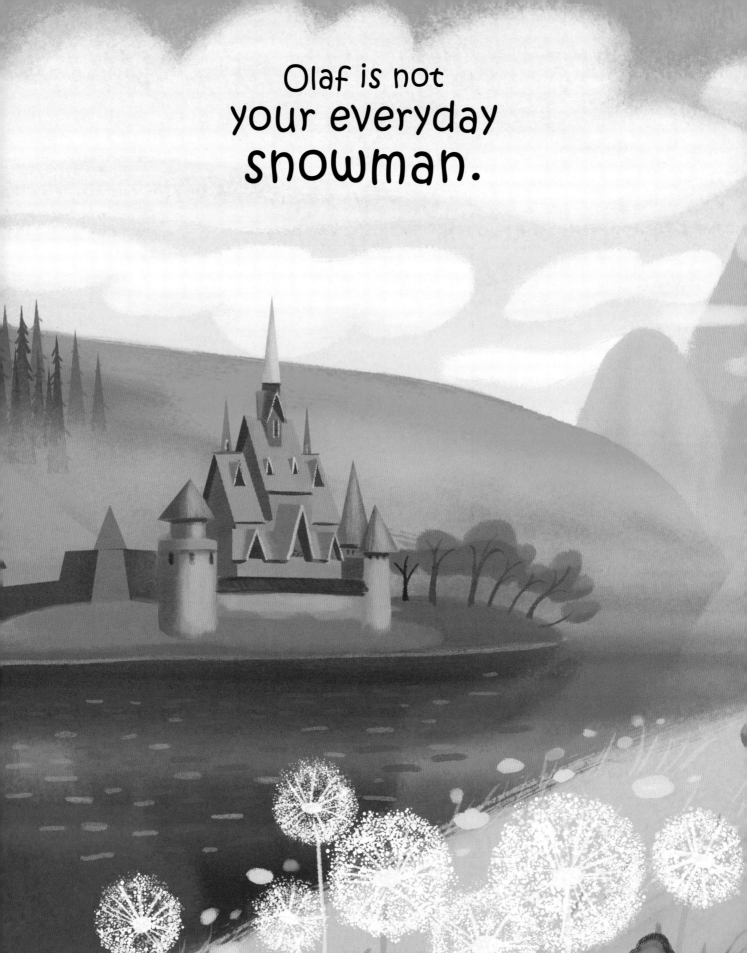

Olaf is not
your everyday
snowman.

He even
sings.

But those aren't the only things
that make him special!

Olaf is special **because**

he sees the **best in EVERYONE.**

His brother,
Marshmallow,
    is a playful
      fellow....

Sven the reindeer
is forever trying to
kiss his nose ...

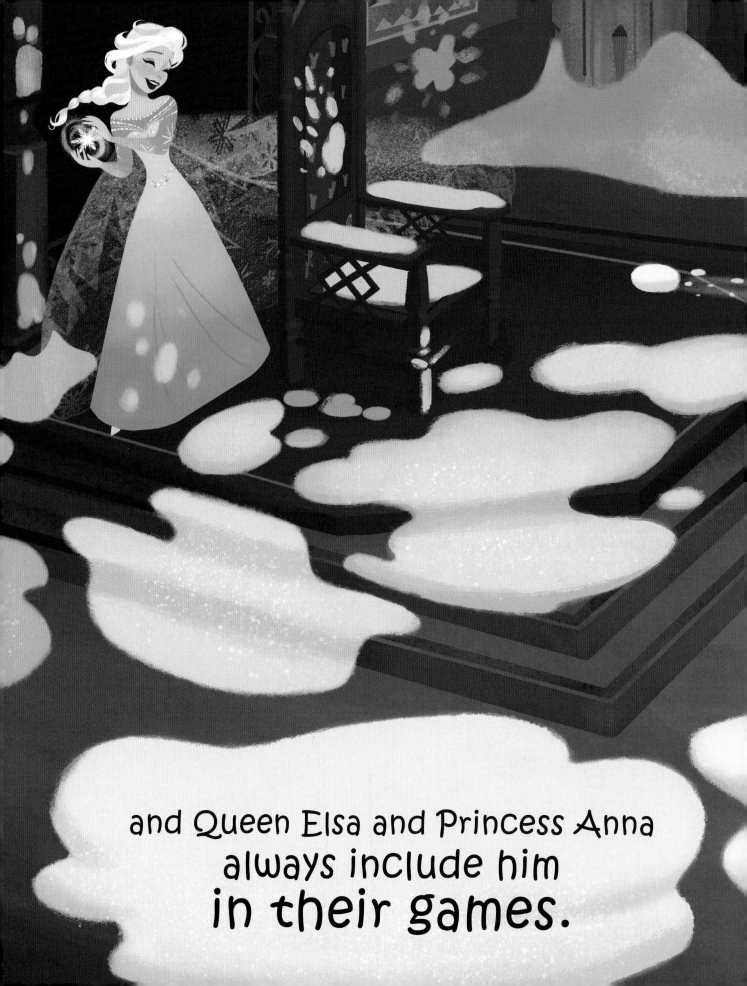

and Queen Elsa and Princess Anna
always include him
in their games.

Olaf is special
because

he finds
beauty in
every day ...

Olaf dreams about sandcastles ...

and ships sailing to new horizons ...

Olaf dreams about soaring in the SKY ...

and picking fresh fruit ...

Olaf is
special
because
in his
eyes,
summer

Or winter,

every day is an adventure ...

and
every
night
shines.

Olaf is
special because
he knows
that every
ending ...

is a chance for a new beginning ...

and
a
Chance ...

for a
nice warm
hug!